Billie B. Brown

www.BillieBBrownBooks.com

Billie B. Brown Books

The Bad Butterfly
The Soccer Star
The Midnight Feast
The Second-best Friend
The Extra-special Helper
The Beautiful Haircut
The Big Sister
The Spotty Vacation
The Birthday Mix-up
The Secret Message
The Little Lie
The Best Project
The Deep End
The Copycat Kid
The Night Fright

First American Edition 2015
Kane Miller, A Division of EDC Publishing

Text copyright © 2012 Sally Rippin
Illustrations copyright © 2012 Aki Fukuoka
First published in Australia in 2012 by Hardie Grant Egmont

For information contact:
Kane Miller, A Division of EDC Publishing
P.O. Box 470663
Tulsa, OK 74147-0663
www.kanemiller.com
www.edcpub.com
www.usbornebooksandmore.com

Library of Congress Control Number: 2014950303

Printed and bound in the United States of America
3 4 5 6 7 8 9 10

ISBN: 978-1-61067-390-7

The
Deep End

By Sally Rippin

Illustrated by Aki Fukuoka

Kane Miller
A DIVISION OF EDC PUBLISHING

Chapter One

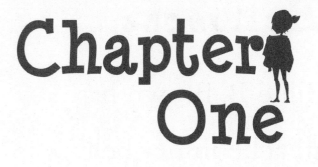

Billie B. Brown has one pair of goggles, one yellow towel and one red bathing suit. Do you know what the "B" in Billie B. Brown stands for?

Bellyache.

Billie B. Brown has an ache in her belly as big as a whale. Today Billie's class is having swimming lessons. Billie loves paddling at the beach, but she hates swimming at the pool.

2

One yellow towel

One pair of goggles

One red bathing suit

The pool is noisy and splashy and deep.

Last year Billie's class had swimming lessons in the little pool. This year they will be in the big pool. When Billie thinks about the deep end of the big pool she feels **sick**.

4

In the bus on the way to
the pool Billie sits next
to Jack. Jack is Billie's
best friend. They always
sit together.

Usually Billie and Jack
talk or sing silly songs, but
today Billie is very quiet.

"Are you OK?" says Jack.

"Of course!" says Billie.
"I have a bit of a tummy
ache, that's all."

Billie doesn't want Jack
to know she is **scared**.
Jack is a good swimmer.

6

If Billie tells Jack she is scared of the deep end, he might think she is silly.

The bus pulls up outside the pool. Everyone in Billie's class cheers so **loudly** that the bus driver has to cover his ears. Everyone except Billie. She shrinks into her seat.

7

8

"OK, class!" Ms. Walton calls out. "Settle down. Do you all have your swimming bags with you?"

"YES!" everyone shouts.

Suddenly Billie has an idea. A super-duper idea! She quickly kicks her swimming bag under the seat in front of her. Then she puts up her hand.

"Um, Ms. Walton, I forgot mine!" she says. "I won't be able to swim today."

"No, you didn't," says Jack. "It's here, under the seat!"

"That's lucky!" Ms. Walton says. "Thank you, Jack."

"Yeah, thanks, Jack," Billie says **glumly**. She follows Jack off the bus.

"I hope we're in the Sharks group together!" Jack says to Billie.

Billie sighs. The class will be put in three groups – Sharks, Stingrays and Swordfish. The Sharks group is the best.

Billie looks at the form her mom has filled in.

Billie knows she is not
good enough to be in the
Sharks group with Jack.
Billie is more like an
octopus than a shark.
Arms and legs everywhere!

Chapter Two

At the swimming center, Billie and her class get ready in the locker rooms. Then they meet Ms. Walton out near the little pool.

Billie sighs. She wishes
her class was still in the
little pool. Even at the
deep end, the water only
goes up to her chin.
But Ms. Walton leads
them over to the big pool.

Next to the big pool
there is a sign that says:
Warning. Deep Water.

Billie feels her heart begin to jump around. She tugs Ms. Walton's arm.

"Yes, Billie?" says Ms. Walton.

"I don't want to go in the big pool," Billie whispers.

"Oh? Why not?" says
Ms. Walton.

"I…I can't swim very well,"
Billie says shyly. She feels
her cheeks burn **hot**.

Ms. Walton smiles and
squeezes Billie's hand.
"Well, that's why we're
here, Billie. To learn!"

"But Jack can already
swim," Billie says.

"And I bet everyone else can too."

Just then, two boys start being silly. Ms. Walton has to rush over to stop them. They might fall into the pool! The rest of the class walk over to the benches.

"Come on, Billie!" says Jack.

Billie flops down on
a bench next to Jack.
She is sure she will be the
worst swimmer in the class.
Everyone will laugh at her.
Or maybe she will
even drown! Billie can't
decide what would be
worse – drowning or
being laughed at?

Soon everyone is standing by the side of the pool. Billie shivers in her scratchy red bathing suit. Next to her, Jack jumps up and down with **excitement**.

Three swimming teachers stand nearby.

"OK" shouts a teacher. "We're going to divide you into three groups. Has everyone been practicing since last year?"

"YES!" everyone yells. Everyone except Billie, of course.

Billie just looks into the deep, deep water and pulls **nervously** at her bathing suit.

"Sharks! Sharks!" Jack whispers to Billie. Billie tries to feel like a shark. Sharks are fast and not afraid of anything. But it is no use. Right now she feels more like a wobbly jellyfish.

Chapter Three

A swimming teacher
reads out names for the
Sharks group. Jack, Tracey
and Benny are all Sharks.
They jump in and swim
away with the teacher.

The next teacher reads

out the Stingrays group.

Mika and Ella are

both Stingrays.

Billie crosses

her fingers

that her name

will be read out,

but the teacher

finishes reading.

The Stingrays swim away with the other teacher.

At first, Billie thinks she is the only person left. She was right. She *is* the worst swimmer in the class.

But wait! Someone else is standing by the side of the pool. Someone with a fancy frilly bathing suit and a pink bathing cap.

Billie sneaks a peek.
It's Lola!

*Does that mean that
Lola can't swim either?*
Billie wonders. *But Lola
is good at everything!*

Even though Lola
and Billie aren't really
friends, Billie feels a little
better. She gives Lola a
shy smile, but Lola just
bites her nails nervously.

"Can't you swim, Lola?"
Billie says.

"So? Can't *you*?" Lola
says crossly.

Billie frowns.

"You don't have to
be mean!" she says.

The swimming teacher
smiles a friendly smile.
"Hey, there!" he says.
"You two must be
my Swordfish."

Billie feels cross.

She doesn't want to be
in a group with Lola.

Maybe if Billie swims
all the way over to the
Sharks, she will prove that
she is good enough to join
them. But if she doesn't
hurry she'll get stuck with
grumpy old Lola.

So, Billie pinches her nose, shuts her eyes tight and... **jumps!**

Down, down, down
Billie sinks. Deep down
into the water.

Oh no! she panics.
I'm going to drown!
Her heart thumps in
her ears. She kicks her
arms and legs, but it's no
use. She only sinks deeper
and deeper into the water.

Billie isn't swimming like a shark at all. She isn't even swimming like a fish! Billie is dropping through the water like a stone.

Chapter Four

Suddenly, Billie feels an arm grab her around the waist. She is jerked out of the water and plonked back onto the side of the pool. The teacher grins at her.

"Perhaps you still need
a little practice?" he says.
He beckons to Lola.
"Come and join us!"

Great! Billie thinks crossly.
She glares at the water,
shivering.

Lola walks over and sits down next to Billie. The two girls don't look at each other.

"Right!" says the teacher. "This time I want you to slide in *slowly* and hold onto the edge of the pool, OK? Then we'll start by practicing some doggie paddle."

Billie is **horrified**.
Oh no! Doggie paddle?
That's for babies, she
thinks. *Everyone will*
definitely laugh at me now.

Suddenly Lola bursts
into tears. Billie looks
at her, surprised.

The teacher looks worried.
"What's wrong with your
friend?" he asks Billie.

"She's not my…" Billie starts, but then she stops. Now that Lola's crying she doesn't seem so mean anymore.

"What's the matter, Lola?" Billie says gently.

Lola looks up at Billie. "I'm a terrible swimmer," she says in a little voice. "I can't even doggie paddle!"

Billie laughs. "Is that all? Don't worry! Doggie paddle is *easy*," she says. "I'll show you."

Lola frowns. "It's all right for you, Billie," she says. "You're good at everything!

Monkey bars, soccer, running…I'm *terrible* at sports!"

"What?" Billie says. "*You're* the one who's good at everything, Lola! Music, spelling, ballet… Remember how bad I was at ballet?"

Lola nods her head. Then she giggles.

"You *were* a pretty bad butterfly."

Lola dries her eyes. "I guess we're good at different things. But we're *both* bad at swimming!"

"No, we're not," says
Billie. "We just have to
learn. Come on!"

Lola sighs. "I don't want
to be in the Swordfish
group. That's the worst
group," she says.

Billie doesn't want to be
in the worst group either.
Just then, she has an idea.
A super-duper idea!

"You're right," says Billie.
She grins. "So let's start
our own group. We can
be the Doggie Paddlers!
Dogs are *much* nicer than
swordfish and sharks."

"The Doggie Paddlers?
I like it!" says the
swimming instructor.

Lola laughs. Billie laughs
too. Then she takes Lola's
hand and the two girls
slide slowly into the water.

And this time Billie isn't
scared at all.

43

Collect them all!